The Borrowed Hanukkah Latkes

Linda Glaser

illustrations by Nancy Cote

ALBERT WHITMAN & COMPANY • MORTON GROVE, ILLINOIS

To Charlotte, who has a heart of gold and who can be "as stubborn as an ox." —L. G.

To my brother, Steve, and sister, Karen, who light the way for me. —N. C.

Library of Congress Cataloging-in-Publication Data

Glaser, Linda.
The borrowed Hanukkah latkes / written by Linda Glaser; illustrated by Nancy Cote.
p. cm.
Summary: A young girl finds a way to include her elderly neighbor in her family's Hanukkah celebration.
ISBN 0-8075-0841-1
[1. Neighborliness—Fiction. 2. Hanukkah—Fiction.]
I. Cote, Nancy, ill. II. Title.
PZ7.G48047Bo 1997
[E]—dc21 96-54022
CIP AC

The paintings were done in gouache and colored pencil.
The text typeface is Quadraat.
The design is by Scott Piehl.

Potato Latkes
(For 5 or 6 people)

6 healthy-sized potatoes
1 egg
1 small onion
3 T. matzo meal, or bread crumbs
1 tsp. salt
oil - enough to almost cover latkes
    in frying pan

Rachel's- Scrub potatoes. Grate the potatoes
part   and onion. Pour off extra liquid.
        Add egg, matzo meal and salt.
        Mix.

Mama's- Drop potato mixture into hot oil
part   with tablespoon. Fry both sides
       until golden brown. Drain on a
       clean towel.

Rachel's- Serve hot with sour cream or
part   applesauce.
        Eat them in good health!

R ACHEL HOPPED ON ONE FOOT, then the other. It was the last night of Hanukkah and all the relatives were coming. Papa got out extra plates. Mama flipped latkes left and right.

"Here." She gave Rachel a latke. "Tell me if it's any good."

Rachel took a bite. *Mmmm.* Mama's potato latkes weren't just good. They were like taking a little trip straight up to heaven.

The phone rang. Mama wiped her hands on her apron.

"Hello! Miriam! Oh...your Aunt Tilly? Sure she can come. And her seven grandchildren? Of course. I'll have plenty of latkes. Don't worry." Mama got off the phone and shook her head. "Eight more people!"

Rachel bounced in the chair. "That makes seventeen, including us."

Mama held her head. "Seventeen people in this tiny house! And less than an hour until they come! Papa! Get more dishes down. Rachel, get more potatoes from the cellar."

Rachel raced downstairs, grabbed the potato sack, and raced back up. Mama opened the sack. "Only three sick little potatoes?"

"That's what's left," said Rachel.

"Oy!" Mama smacked her forehead. "This is bad. It's too late to go to the store."

"Maybe we can borrow some from Mrs. Greenberg," said Rachel.

"No." Mama shook her head. "It wouldn't be right. She's all alone. Every year I invite her. She won't come! She thinks she'd be a bother. But she always says, 'If you need anything, just let me know.' She's got a heart of gold, but she's as stubborn as an ox."

"Maybe she'll come if we borrow her potatoes," said Rachel.

"Good idea," said Mama. "Quick. Go ask."

Rachel raced next door. Mrs. Greenberg's house was always clean and tidy, like its face was just scrubbed and its blouse was tucked in, while Rachel's house always looked like it was still in its pajamas and needed to brush its hair yet.

Rachel knocked. The door swung open.

"Well, well, well! Look who's here. Come in, come in."

When Mrs. Greenberg smiled, it was with her whole face.

Rachel stepped inside. Everything was still. It didn't seem much like Hanukkah—except for the menorah, with candles waiting.

"Sit down. I don't charge extra." Mrs. Greenberg winked.

Rachel shook her head. "I can't stay. Mama's making latkes. Can we borrow some potatoes?"

"Borrow?" Mrs. Greenberg frowned. "No." She rushed off and soon returned with a big sack. "Here. Don't borrow. I don't want them back. You all should eat them in good health."

"Thank you," said Rachel. "And now, please come. We want you with us."

Mrs. Greenberg was silent. So silent you could hear the walls listening. You could hear the rug holding its breath.

"Rachel, dear," she finally said. "Your mama has enough tumult without me. All those latkes. All that work. I know how it is. Years ago, every Hanukkah, my house was filled with people, too. But those days are long gone." She smoothed down her apron. "Now you go home. And happy Hanukkah."

Rachel dragged her feet home. She set the sack on the counter.

"Wonderful!" said Mama.

"Not so wonderful," said Rachel. "Mrs. Greenberg won't come."

"Didn't I tell you?" said Mama. "She has a heart of gold, but she's as stubborn as an ox. Now, quick, get the rest of the eggs for the latkes."

Rachel looked in the refrigerator. "There aren't any left."

"Oy!" Mama smacked her forehead. "This is bad."

Rachel nodded. "I'll go ask Mrs. Greenberg."

"No!" Mama shook her head. "It's not right."

"We have to," said Rachel. "And now she'll *have* to come."

Rachel ran over. "Can we borrow some eggs for the latkes?"

"Borrow?" Mrs. Greenberg shook her finger at Rachel. She handed her a carton of eggs. "Don't borrow. Use them in good health."

"Thank you," said Rachel. "And now, *please* come for Hanukkah."

"Thanks anyway," said Mrs. Greenberg. "But honestly, I'm more comfortable right here in my own house."

Back at home, Rachel set the eggs on the counter. "Mrs. Greenberg *still* won't come. Maybe I'll take her some latkes."

"Don't," said Mama. "No one wants to eat Hanukkah latkes alone."

That minute, the doorbell rang. Aunts, uncles, and cousins poured in—all hugging, kissing, laughing, and crowding around!

But when it was time to eat, no one sat down. There weren't enough chairs.

"I'll get some crates from the cellar," said Papa.

What was Papa thinking? To sit on crates and eat latkes?

"Wait!" said Rachel. "I have an idea."

She ran straight to Mrs. Greenberg's house. "Can we borrow some chairs?"

"Of course. Take what you need."

One by one, Rachel carried the chairs to Mrs. Greenberg's front door. Then she stopped. "Oh! I just thought—but no. I shouldn't ask for anything else."

"Ask!" said Mrs. Greenberg. "Whatever it is, I want you to have it."

"All right," said Rachel. "We need room for all these chairs."

"Room? What do you mean, room?" asked Mrs. Greenberg.

Rachel tried not to smile. "You have lots of room."

Mrs. Greenberg looked at Rachel. "You mean your guests should come and sit in my house?"

"That would be nice," said Rachel.

Mrs. Greenberg was quiet for a long time. So long that the walls got tired of waiting. And the rug couldn't hold its breath anymore.

Finally she spoke. "Rachel, my dear, someday when you're an old lady like me, I hope you have a girl living right next door who's as smart and sweet as you. I'd love to have some company for Hanukkah."

Rachel threw her arms around her.

Mrs. Greenberg hugged her back. "Rachel, you have a heart of gold. But did anyone ever tell you you're as stubborn as an ox?"

"No," said Rachel. "But thank you. And the same to you."

"Me?" Mrs. Greenberg laughed. "You're worse than me, Rachel. I didn't think it was possible."

So everyone trooped over with plates full of latkes.
Rachel marched over with two plates.

She handed one to Mrs. Greenberg.

"Here," said Rachel. "Don't borrow. Just eat them in good health."